For all the unsung heroes

With thanks to our readers:

Michael Martin

Nick Rees

Hayden Smith

Contents

Chapter 1

The Children's Home

This is a true story.

It's all about a boy called Walter. He grew up and had an amazing life.

He became a professional footballer. He fought in the First World War. He changed the world. And then he was forgotten.

Here he is in a family photo.

Walter with his family. Walter is the boy in the middle of the front row.

His mother is not in this picture because, just two weeks before Walter's seventh birthday, she died. His brothers and sisters are in the picture and so is his dad.

Walter's dad was called Daniel. Daniel was the son of slaves – yes, slaves.

Daniel was born in Barbados. He was the first free man in his family and he worked hard to learn how to be a carpenter. Then he set sail for England and he landed and lived in Folkestone, married a local girl called Alice – Walter's mum – and they had the children you can see in this picture.

The hero of this story is the boy sitting down in the middle of this photo. His full name was Walter John Daniel Tull and he was born on 28 April 1888.

1888 was a very long time ago and people had different lives back then – and, as you can see, they wore different clothes.

Doctors and hospitals and medicine were not so advanced in those days, and by the time Walter was nine, his father had also died. Yes, Walter Tull was an orphan.

After his father died, Walter's family was split up and he and his brother Edward were sent away to be looked after in a Children's Home.

The Children's Home was in the East End of London – far away from where Walter had grown up. Walter didn't have any friends in London. All he had was his brother, Edward.

*

It was hard to get used to the sounds and the smells of a town like London. And some of the other kids were mean.

Walter and Edward looked different. They were the only two black boys in a Children's

Walter's class at Bonner Road Children's Home.

Home full of white kids. Some of the bigger kids made fun of them. One of the biggest kids was Harry.

Harry took every chance to make life hard for the new kids. He was a bully.

Walter is third from the right in the front row.

Other kids stayed away from Walter and Edward – they didn't want to get on the wrong side of Harry.

One day someone sent a box of apples into the Home. "So what?!" you're thinking. "Apples! Big deal!" But it was a big deal to the kids in the Home. It was a very big deal.

The kids were told they could have just one apple each and the big kids (Harry's gang) could have the extra "windfalls".

Walter picked his apple. "What's a windfall?" he asked.

"A windfall is an apple that's fallen to the ground," Edward told him.

"So if an apple falls to the ground, it's mine!" said Harry, and he stuck out his long leg and tripped little Walter up.

The small boy went flying and so did the apple. Up into the air it went and Harry waited for it to fall to the ground so he could have it.

But the apple never landed on the ground.

Walter stuck his foot out and the apple landed on his toe. Then he flicked it to his knee and passed it from knee to knee, foot to foot, onto his head, onto his back and then onto his head again. Harry made a grab for it but Walter was too quick for him. Walter was only little but he was already brilliant at this game of keepy-uppy. He could do it for ages.

All the other kids came round to watch.

They were clapping and slapping Walter on the back. "Show us how to do that!" they said.

That was how Walter got his apple – and he also got the respect of all the other kids.

He and Edward had friends now and Harry gave up picking on them. Sorted!

The Children's Home was run by the Church. The staff made sure the kids knew right from wrong. The staff fed the kids and gave them clothes to wear. They sent the kids to lessons and they trained them to work. But it wasn't like having a real mum and dad.

Walter and Edward looked after each other as best they could but it can't have been easy for them.

They had known a life with a mum and a dad to look after them. They had lived in a family house, by the sea, and now here they were in the East End of London where they knew no one.

It was just the two of them in a strange new world.

Then, in 1900, the boys were separated. Edward was adopted by a family who lived in Glasgow in Scotland and Walter was left on his own at the Children's Home in London.

Chapter 2

Football

Walter and Edward *did* keep in touch. All the Tull children wrote letters and postcards to each other. But of course they could not phone each other in those days.

Things were very different back then.

Here are some of the things that were different for Walter and the other children in the Home.

- They had no mobile phones.

- They had no phones at all.

- They had no TV.

- No internet.

- They had no computers.

- No games consoles.

- No hot showers and baths.

- No proper heating.

The kids were often very cold. They were nearly always hungry.

Here's some of the things they DID have.

- Horses clip-clopping on the cobblestones.

- Gas lamps on the streets.

- Kids dying of hunger and disease.

- Long hours of work and strict teachers who were allowed to beat the children with sticks or straps.

But some things were the same.

The kids were all mad about football.

They played in the streets. The kids could get up a footie team in no time at all. Walter was their star.

Walter was always kicking a ball.

If he didn't have a ball, he kicked stones. If he didn't have stones, he kicked bits of rag. Or tins. Or boxes. Or anything! And boy, could he hit the ball! He could dribble. He could pass. He could tackle. And he could score.

The kids made up a Children's Home team and he was their star player. They always made him Captain and everyone wanted to be on his team.

He was a good Captain. He had brilliant football skills and he was a brilliant leader too. He was fair. He didn't lose his temper. All the kids respected him.

Walter in the Bonner Road football team. He is second from the left in the front row.

And boy, he could play!

Oh, you talk of your stars now. The ones who are paid millions and millions of pounds. But Walter was as good as the best of them. Walter was better than the best.

The kids in the Home knew he was good but one day they knew for sure. He was spotted by a scout for a local team.

It was an amateur team. They were called Clapton FC and they were the best team in the area.

When Clapton picked Walter to play for them, the other kids in his Children's Home team were as proud as proud can be. They went on and on about it to everyone – to anyone – who would listen.

They told all the other kids they met. They told all the other kids at the Children's Home (of course). They told everyone at school. They told the baker, the coalman. They told passers-by. They showed off to anyone who would listen.

Walter didn't go round shouting about it.
He was never the type to show off. But he had
plenty he could have shown off about.

Clapton FC was an amateur team but they
were the best. The very best. With Walter
playing for them, they won everything. Walter
Tull had become a famous name.

Finlayson Family Archive

The Clapton FC team with their winners' cups.
Walter is second from the right in the front row.

Clapton won the FA Amateur Cup – the top prize in amateur football. And they won it 6–0!

They won everything. They won the London Senior Cup. And they won the London County Amateur Cup. They really were the best.

When Walter was picked to play for them, he was called "the catch of the season".

But this was only the start.

His talent was soon spotted by a bigger club. This time by a professional team. Tottenham Hotspur – yes, the Spurs! Walter Tull played for Spurs.

W.D.Tull.
Tottenham Hotspur.

Walter wearing his Spurs kit.

Chapter 3

Star!

Walter was the very first black out-field player in professional football. A star!

He got a signing-on fee of ten pounds and a wage of four pounds a week – this was a good wage at the time!

Bit by bit everyone – the other Spurs players and the Spurs fans – came to like and admire this strong, proud man. He earned their respect.

Finlayson Family Archive

Walter, on the left, playing for Spurs against Manchester United.

● RESPECT ●

Walter's very first match for Spurs was in 1909. It was Spurs' first game after they went up to the top division. Walter ran onto that field and he played like a dream. He played in front of a crowd of 30,000 cheering fans.

He was brilliant. Everyone said so. He could pass the ball 35 yards right to the winger's feet. The newspapers all said he was the star of the team. His future was bright. Very bright. But later that year something happened.

He was playing at an away match at Bristol City when it started.

Every time the ball went near him, the Bristol crowd started to yell at him. They couldn't have a go at him for his playing – so they got at him because he was black.

They made up rude songs about him. They spat at him. Every time he got the ball, they made monkey noises.

There he was standing in the middle of that huge football ground – the only black face in a sea of white. All around him people hissed and spat and shouted.

It must have seemed like a nightmare. This had never happened before in football. It shocked Walter. It shocked the rest of the team too. It even shocked newspaper reporters.

6

"They're just a bunch of fools and idiots!" said one of Walter's team-mates. "Don't let them get to you."

"Who do they think they are to pick on you?!" said another team-mate. "You're ten times better than they could ever dream of being."

"Just a bunch of fools," the team agreed.

"Don't let them get to you!"

Chapter 4

A New Start

Walter put his faith in fairness, hard work and kindness. He always stood up strong and proud but what happened at Bristol did get to him. He felt sick about it.

He almost lost his nerve. He didn't play much for the rest of the season.

He spoke about it a lot. He thought about it a lot. He went over and over it but he couldn't get to grips with it. It's hard to come to terms with something so unfair. But there is a saying, "What doesn't kill you makes you stronger." Walter pulled himself together bit by bit and made a new start.

The next season he took a transfer to another team. He went to Northampton Town. They were a BIG team back then. Things change! Northampton paid a very big transfer fee for him.

He soon became the star of his new team. He played 110 games and was their most popular player.

His brother Edward was proud of him. But by this time Edward was living far away.

Remember, he had been adopted. The family who adopted him lived in Scotland. So that's where he was – up in Scotland – far, far from Northampton and his famous brother.

They kept in touch. But one day Walter was offered a wonderful chance – the chance of a transfer to Rangers.

That is Glasgow Rangers – so Walter would be just around the corner from his brother!

Both Walter and Edward were over the moon at the idea of living near each other again and Rangers were over the moon at the chance of having Walter Tull to play for them. He was the best! Everything was going to be *brilliant*.

But then, in the summer of 1914, war broke out.

Chapter 5

War

Walter was now known as Private Walter Tull. He was just a plain soldier. He had been one of the first to sign up to fight for his country in the First World War.

He joined the 17th Middlesex Regiment – the Football Battalion. Many of the other members of the Regiment were also footballers.

● RESPECT ●

Walter played his last football match in the autumn of 1915. In November he was in France, ready to fight.

He didn't know much about war. But he soon found out.

The first thing he learned was how to march. Then he was marched off into the middle of nowhere. He started in France.

The men lived in muddy freezing trenches in the ground.

In the trenches it was cold. It was wet. It was boring. It was alive with rats and fleas. And it was muddy.

You spent your time lying in mud, sleeping in mud, soaked in mud. Some men even drowned in mud.

And when you popped your head up out of the trench – you got shot at.

Men were killed every day.

In October 1916, Walter's regiment was sent to the Somme. This was the worst battle of the war and he was in it.

Everett Historical/shutterstock.com

Back at home, Edward read about it in the newspapers and in Walter's letters, and later, much later, he read about it in the history books. And still Edward found it hard to believe.

Hard to imagine.

● RESPECT ●

You try it.

On one morning in the battle of the Somme this is what happened.

Nearly 20,000 (twenty thousand) British men were killed.

Over 35,000 (yes, that's right – thirty-five thousand) men were wounded.

Five hundred and eighty-five men were captured alive. Many were just listed as "missing". This could mean they were found dead and no one knew who they were. Or they were blown up into small pieces. Or they simply sank into holes in the mud.

In all, nearly 60,000 men were killed, wounded or lost – in just one morning.

That's about the same number of men as a sell-out crowd at Spurs' new home ground.

Think of it.

Sixty thousand men lost and what did they win? They won a few yards of mud.

Wounded soldiers on stretchers waiting to be carried to safety.

Chapter 6

Wounded

There has never been a battle like the Somme.
Never. And Walter was there. He survived
it. He survived a nightmare of blood and mud,
guns crashing, men screaming, friends dying.
Not only did he survive – he did well. He kept
a cool head. He looked after all those around
him. He became a leader.

The officers praised him for keeping his cool. They said he was one of the bravest men they had ever met. In a later report they said he should have a medal.

He had to fight in other battles too. In France and in Italy he fought on until he was wounded and sent off to hospital.

When he got back to England, something surprising happened.

In those days – and still today – there was a huge difference between officers and plain soldiers. Officers had been to posh schools and were often rich. "Men", or plain soldiers, didn't often get the chance to become officers and in those days black men were just not allowed to become officers. There was an army law against it.

But they broke that law for Walter Tull.

So when he went back to the battlefield, he went back as an officer. Walter Tull was the first ever black officer in the British army.

Walter, now known as 2nd Lieutenant Walter Tull, in his officer's uniform.

It's true. You can look it up in the history books. Walter, the grandson of a slave, a poor orphan who had to make his own way in the world, became the first black man to lead white men into battle.

Finlayson Family Archive

Walter visited his brother Edward in Scotland when he was there for officer training. Walter is the man standing on the right.

Chapter 7

1918

It was the year 1918. This was the year that the war ended, but just before the end of the war Walter Tull was shot.

It was one of the final battles of the war. Walter and his men had been ordered to leave their trench and go "over the top" towards the enemy.

Over the top they went. Shells crashed around them, bullets rained down on them. Then, suddenly, Walter was on the ground. He had been shot.

He fell into the mud in the middle of the battlefield, between the British and the German lines. They called this place "No Man's Land". There was very little chance of saving anyone who fell here.

But to his men, Walter was not just an officer. He was a real friend.

They ran to his rescue. They ran through a hail of bullets. They ran through exploding shells but they couldn't get to him.

They tried again. And again. And again. They tried their best but they couldn't save

Finlayson Family Archive

Walter in his uniform, on the left, with some fellow officers.

him. Walter died. His body was never found. Never buried.

Edward learned of all this in a letter sent to him by the Officer in Charge. The officer said Walter Tull had been one of the bravest and most popular men he'd ever met. "The army has lost a faithful officer," he wrote, "and we have lost a friend."

Walter was awarded the British War Medal and the Victory Medal. He was recommended for a Military Cross but this has still not been granted to him.

Col André Kritzinger/Public Domain; Osioni/Public Domain; MOD/Open Government Licence

From left to right: the British War Medal, Victory Medal and Military Cross

Chapter 8

The End

So that's how the grandson of a slave grew up to become the first black officer in the British army.

He fought in the Somme and survived to fight there again. Not many soldiers could say that.

He won medals in the war and he won medals in football. He played for some of the best teams in the country.

He looked after his team-mates on the football field. He looked after his men on the battlefield.

He was a strong, proud man.

A hero.

This story is true. Parts of it may be hard to imagine. Parts of it may be hard to believe, especially now our world is very different.

What would Walter think about the world we live in now? What would he think about the things that have changed and the things that have stayed the same? What would he say if he could talk to us?

And what would you say if you met him now? I bet I know what you'd say.

"Respect!"

Text of the memorial

Through his actions W. D. J. Tull
ridiculed the barriers of ignorance
that tried to deny people of colour
equality with their contemporaries.
His life stands testament to a
determination to confront those
people and those obstacles that
sought to diminish him and the
World in which he lived.
It reveals a man though rendered
breathless in his prime, whose
strong heart still beats loudly.

Walter Tull's memorial in Northampton.

Author's Note

Respect was first published in 2005 and written and researched some time before that. It has gathered attention, awards, reviews and many, many readers. It has gone through many changes including different covers, changes in illustration and text, and finally the inclusion of photographs – even more photographs in this edition!

When I started writing and researching this book, there was very little information

available about Walter Tull, but as the years
passed his fame has grown and now there
are other books and plenty of background
information on the Internet. Readers contacted
me. Often it was to ask further questions about
Walter; very often it was to say things along
the lines of "I don't usually like reading – but I
loved this book!" Sometimes it was to question
my information – and those who questioned
it were right. I had indeed made a mistake
in the first version of the book. I got the age
of Walter's brother Edward wrong. Edward
was older than Walter. In my first telling of
Walter's story I described Edward as Walter's
little brother.

I alerted readers to this mistake when I
visited schools and gave talks, and suggested
that they learn from my mistake and always
check, using multiple sources. You can't believe

everything you read on the Internet – or in a book. People make mistakes.

I have had the chance to correct that error in this new edition. I also have the wonderful opportunity of telling you that Walter – from being almost completely unknown – has now become more and more famous. There have been more books, including *Walter Tull's Scrapbook*, which I wrote. There has been radio and television coverage, plans to make a film and, in commemoration of the centenary of the First World War, in 2015 a special £5 coin was made – with an image of Walter Tull on it. Then in 2018, a hundred years after Walter's death, a new first-class stamp was issued that featured Walter Tull.

He still has no gravestone dedicated to him and has never received the Military Cross medal for which he was recommended but he has earned memorials, acknowledgement and respect in other ways.

Walter is a fine example of resilience. He was a hero – the first black professional out-field footballer and the first black British officer. Since his death there have been many changes but not all the battles are won. In 1909 Walter suffered racist abuse on the football pitch. Over 100 years later that abuse still continues. In 2019 the organisation Kick it Out celebrated 25 years of fighting racism and the fight for equality still continues.